For George Williams

First published 2009 by Walker Books Ltd
87 Vauxhall Walk, London SE11 5HJ

2 4 6 8 10 9 7 5 3 1

This book has been typeset in Gill Sans MT Schoolbook.

Printed in China.

British Library Cataloguing in Publication Data:
a catalogue record for this book is available
from the British Library.

ISBN 978-1-4063-0909-6

www.walker.co.uk

Tilly and
her friends
all live
together in
a little yellow
house...

Goodnight
Tiptoe

Polly Dunbar

WALKER BOOKS
AND SUBSIDIARIES
LONDON · BOSTON · SYDNEY · AUCKLAND

Hector yawned.

Tilly yawned.

Everybody

yawned! Everybody except Tiptoe.

"It's time
for bed,"
said Hector,
snuggling up.

Tilly gave Tiptoe a kiss goodnight.
"I'm not sleepy,"
he said.

Tilly helped put Pru's rollers in.

"Look who's not in bed," said Pru.

"I'm still not sleepy," said Tiptoe. "I don't want to go to bed."

"You can stay up while I clean Doodle's teeth," said Tilly. "Then it's back to bed."

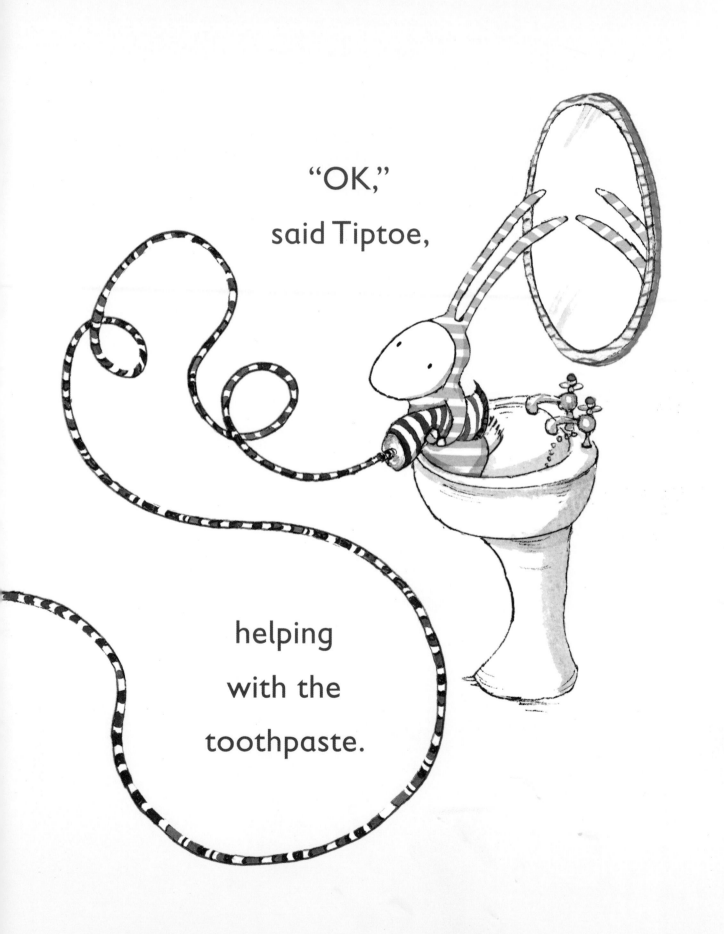

"OK,"
said Tiptoe,

helping
with the
toothpaste.

"Now it **really** is
time for bed," said Tilly.

She sang a lovely lullaby.

TRA LA LA LA

BOOM!
BOOM!
BOOM!

"I'm wide awake!"

When Tilly
had settled Tiptoe
down again,
she helped Tumpty
with his bath.

"I want a story," said Tiptoe.

So Tilly read
a bedtime
story.

Everybody felt very, very, sleepy.

Even Tiptoe closed his eyes.

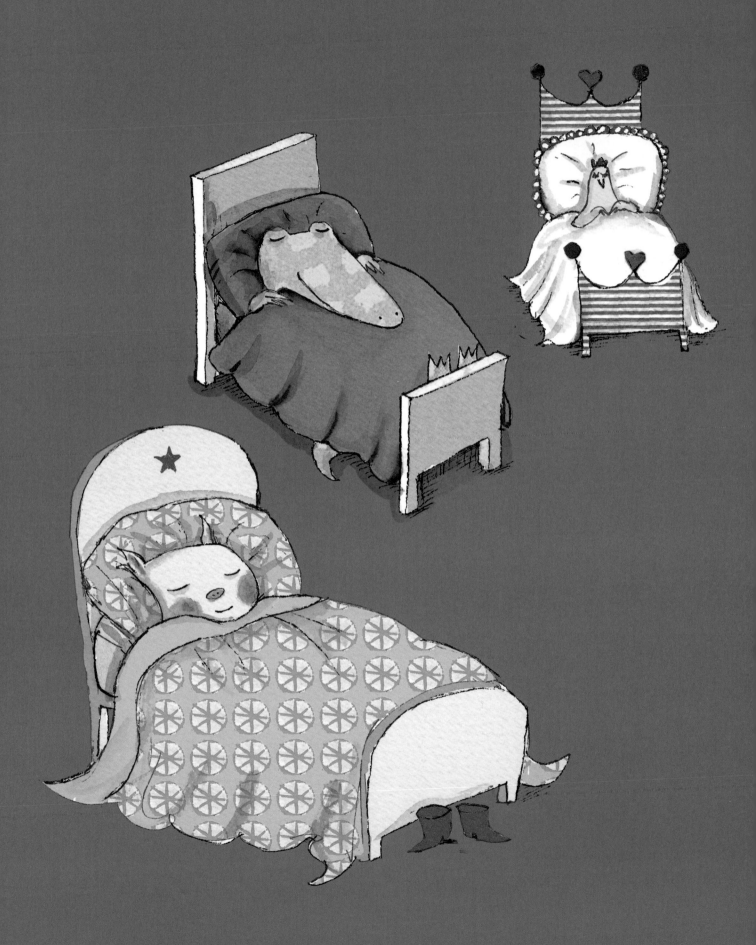

"Sssssshhhh!" whispered Tilly.

"I feel sleepy now,"
said Tilly.
"It must be my bedtime too."
She cleaned her teeth
all by herself.

Tilly got into bed
all by herself.
"Who's going to tuck **me** in?"
she said.
"Who's going to kiss
me goodnight?"

"I am!"
said
Tiptoe.

Goodnight! x